MAGICAL
TALES OF
IRELAND

MAGICAL TALES OF *IRELAND*

HUTCHINSON

London Sydney Auckland Johannesburg

MAGICAL TALES OF IRELAND
A HUTCHINSON BOOK 0 09 176849 7

Published in Great Britain by Hutchinson,
an imprint of Random House Children's Books

This edition published 2003

1 3 5 7 9 10 8 6 4 2

Compiled by Madeleine Nicklin
Text and illustrations copyright © individual authors and illustrators, 2003

RANDOM HOUSE CHILDREN'S BOOKS
61–63 Uxbridge Road, London W5 5SA
A division of The Random House Group Ltd

RANDOM HOUSE AUSTRALIA (PTY) LTD
20 Alfred Street, Milsons Point, Sydney,
New South Wales 2061, Australia

RANDOM HOUSE NEW ZEALAND LTD
18 Poland Road, Glenfield, Auckland 10, New Zealand

RANDOM HOUSE (PTY) LTD
Endulini, 5A Jubilee Road, Parktown 2193, South Africa

THE RANDOM HOUSE GROUP Limited Reg. No. 954009
www.kidsatrandomhouse.co.uk

A CIP catalogue record for this book is available from the British Library.

Printed in Hong Kong

Contents

The Henny Penny Tree

STORY BY SIOBHÁN PARKINSON

ILLUSTRATED BY PAM SMY

O F all the family that lived under the mountain, Littlest was the littlest. Tall One knew everything. Middling knew most things. Littlest didn't know much at all, or so her sisters told her.

One day, Great-Uncle Fergus came clumping over
the mountain in his seven-league boots. Clump,
clump, clump, he came, seven leagues at a time.

Mother came running out to meet him.

'Give those boots a rest, Fergus,' she yelled as he clumped
by, 'or you'll be in England before you know where you are,
and then where'll you be?'

'England,' said Uncle Fergus.

'Yes,' said Mother, 'and wet with it. There's a sea between here and England, I'll have you know.'

Great-Uncle Fergus didn't argue. He sat down on a handy rock and rested his feet in his seven-league boots.

Tall One was the first out of the house after Mother. She brought a big fat hunk of chocolate cake (the kind with cherry jam in the middle) for Great-Uncle Fergus.

'Aren't you the grand girl?' said Uncle Fergus, chomping on the cake, and he gave her a bright gold sovereign all for herself.

'Don't spend it all in the one shop,' he warned her. 'It's pure gold.'

Middling came out next, with a steaming mug of tea for Great-Uncle Fergus, to wash down the chocolate cake.

'Aren't you the finest?' said Great-Uncle Fergus, and he gave her a gleaming silver shilling for herself. 'It's pure silver,' he said. 'Don't spend it all in the one shop.'

Littlest couldn't think what she could do for Great-Uncle Fergus to make him feel welcome. She sat in the house for a long time, and thought and thought. In the end, she came out with a peppermint for Great-Uncle Fergus.

'Well, now,' said Uncle Fergus, 'aren't you the wise one? You knew I'd be feeling a bit cluttered up on the inside with all that chocolate cake, didn't you? And so you brought me a nice digestive peppermint so I won't get the hiccups.

That is the best idea that anyone has had all day.' And he popped the peppermint into his mouth and began to suck it.

'My goodness,' he said then. 'I nearly forgot.' And Great-Uncle Fergus dug deep into his pocket and brought out a shiny copper penny and gave it to Littlest.

'It's pure copper,' he said. 'Don't spend it . . .'

'I know!' said Littlest, jumping up and down, '. . . all in the one shop.'

'No,' said Great-Uncle Fergus. 'That's not what I was going to say.'

'What *were* you going to say?' asked Littlest.

'Do you know what it is?' said Great-Uncle Fergus. 'I forget.'

And he stood up in his seven-league boots, because it was time to clump off home again.

'Oh,' said Littlest. She felt a bit disappointed, but she didn't show it. She didn't want Great-Uncle Fergus to think that she was ungrateful for the penny.

Tall One took her bright gold sovereign to the bank and the bank people gave her lots of real money for it and she bought a beautiful doll and a lot of pink things for her to wear and she was very happy.

Middling took her gleaming silver shilling to the bank and the bank people said, 'You don't get many of those any more,' and they gave her some proper money for it and she bought a book and she was quite happy.

The others didn't think much of Littlest's shiny copper penny.

'It's got a mother hen on it,' Littlest pointed out proudly, 'and lots of dotey little chicks.'

'A penny's a penny,' they said, 'and a penny's all you get for a peppermint and a peppermint's all you get for a penny.'

But Littlest loved her shiny copper penny. It's *treasure*, she said to herself. I wish Great-Uncle Fergus could remember what he was going to say I was not to do with the penny, but in the meantime, I am going to do what you do with treasure. I am going to bury it.

So one day when Tall One and Middling were at school, Littlest took her shiny copper penny out into the yard and she sat on the rock where Great-Uncle Fergus had rested that day in his seven-league boots in case he clumped off to England by mistake and got drowned on the way, and she dug a little hole in the earth and popped her penny into it.

'Now,' she said to the penny, 'you'll be safe until Great-Uncle Fergus remembers.'

When the others came home from school they noticed that Littlest didn't have her shiny copper penny any more.

'What did you buy with your silly henny penny?' they asked her.

'Nothing,' said Littlest.

'But where is it, then?' they asked. 'Did you put it in the bank?'

'No,' said Littlest.

'You've lost it, so,' said Tall One.

'No,' said Littlest.

'Bet you have,' said Middling.

'No!' said Littlest. 'I buried it, to keep it safe.'

Her sisters laughed and laughed. 'You know nothing!' they jeered. 'It'll just go green and mouldy underground and they won't give you anything for it at the bank.'

One week later, when Tall One and Middling and Littlest were eating their breakfast, Mother whisked the

curtains open to let the sun into the kitchen. 'It's so dark in here,' she muttered.

The sisters looked out of the window to see the sun coming in, but what they saw instead of the sun was a big tree trunk filling up almost all the window.

They ran out into the yard to see what was going on, and there beside Great-Uncle Fergus's rock was the most enormous tree you ever saw, bigger than a beech tree, bigger than an oak tree, bigger than a chestnut tree. Just then a breeze whispered through the yard and the leaves of the tree . . . tinkled!

Tinkling leaves! How could that be? Well, this is how it could be: every single leaf on the enormous tree was a shiny copper penny with a mother hen and lots of dotey chicks on it.

'There must be thousands of them!' whispered Tall One.

'Millions!' murmured Middling.

'We're rich!' shouted Littlest, and she ran up to the tree and pulled a handful of leaves off and threw them in the air and they tinkled and pinkled and clinked and chinked and clattered and rattled to the ground. As soon as they did, new penny-leaves sprouted where they had been pulled off. The tree was an unending source of shiny copper coins.

'I wish I'd buried my bright gold sovereign,' said Tall One. 'Gold's worth more than copper.'

'I wish I'd buried my gleaming silver shilling,' said Middling. 'Silver's worth more than copper.'

'It doesn't matter!' cried Littlest. 'I buried my shiny copper penny, and now we have so much copper we'll have to take it in truckloads to the bank. We're rich! Where's Great-Uncle Fergus?'

'In England,' said Mother, coming out of the house behind them. 'He clumped seven leagues too far and landed in the middle of the sea and got his ankles wet and I'm sure he is going to have a sore throat. That man is *such* a worry to me.'

'Don't worry, Mother,' said Tall One. 'Littlest can make him better with a peppermint.' And Middling agreed.

Which just goes to show, thought Littlest, that really Tall One and Middling didn't know very much after all. Peppermint is for tummies. *Honey* is for colds.

Jacinta's Seaside

STORY BY

MARILYN MCLAUGHLIN

ILLUSTRATED BY

LOUISE MANSFIELD

JACINTA dropped her music box into the sea, and when Dad got it out there was no more music in it – just one little scratchy sound and then nothing.

'Why did you bring it to the beach?' Mum asked.

'I wanted my mermaid to hear it,' Jacinta said.

'Well it's no good for music now,' Dad said. 'It's full of sea water and sand.'

'I'm still going to keep it,' Jacinta said.

Jacinta always wanted to keep everything.

She kept all the things she found on the beaches and brought them back to the holiday house at Carrowtrasna.

'Jacinta,' said Mum, 'why is your bed full of stones?'

'They might be seagull eggs. I'm keeping them warm, to see if they hatch.'

'Jacinta!' said Mum. 'What is that awful smell?'

'It's my extra smelly seaweed, from Sweet Nelly's Bay.'

'Put it outside, right now.'

'I want to keep it.'

'OK, but only at the bottom of the garden.'

'Jacinta. Why was this pointy shell on the sofa? I sat on it!'

'That's my special shell which you can hear the sea in. Hold it to your ear.'

It was one of those fat white shells that whirls round into a tiny point, like soft ice cream.

'Put it outside,' Mum said.

'I need to keep it. My mermaid gave me that,' Jacinta said.

'Jacinta,' said Mum, 'have you ever seen this mermaid?'

'No, but that doesn't mean she isn't there.'

Jacinta put the mermaid's shell back on the shelf with all her other seaside things. She had knobbly driftwood that looked like a dragon. She had a white clean mystery bone that might have come from a whale, and maybe once swam around at the bottom of the sea. She had a whole bottle that was not broken and might have had a message in it. She had cockle shells, whelk shells, mussel shells and limpets by the dozen.

When Mum said that the holiday was over and it was time to pack and go home, Jacinta put all her seaside things in her bag.

'Jacinta,' Mum said, 'you can't bring the whole beach home! There isn't room in the car.'

'I want to keep the holidays,' Jacinta said.

'We'll be back next year,' said Mum.

Then Mum saw Jacinta's sad face and said, 'Why not keep just one thing. Put it in your old music box. And don't pick anything smelly.'

Jacinta chose the mermaid's shell for the music box, because it fitted best, and then crammed it in with all her books and toys and shoes. There was just enough room for her in the back seat of the car, on top of two pillows, wedged in by a rolled-up duvet and the golf clubs. The boot was full of suitcases. There was a bike tied on behind and fishing rods and more suitcases on top. Poor car, thought Jacinta. Poor me. Bye-bye Carrowtrasna, bye-bye sea, bye-bye seagulls, bye-bye light house, bye-bye ice-cream shop, bye-bye holidays, bye-bye mermaid.

On the way home, Mum said that she wanted to get chips. That would do for dinner. That cheered Jacinta up. They parked at the sea front and ate the hot chips with their fingers. Jacinta loved eating chips in the car. She gave a big sniff. The vinegar smell flew up her nose and she sneezed. *Atchoo!*

'Bless you! Maybe you're taking a cold, Jacinta,' Mum said.

Dad started to wind up the window of the car.

'No,' Jacinta said. 'I want to keep the smell of the sea. Atchoo!'

It wasn't too bad getting home. Clare from next door was out in the street and Jacinta left all her bags in her bedroom and went out to play. The next morning Mum took her to the shops to buy new shoes for school.

Jacinta sniffed the rubbery smell of the shoes and then she sneezed again.

'I think you're definitely taking a cold, Jacinta, with all this sneezing,' said Mum and she made Jacinta go to bed for the afternoon with a drink of hot orange juice.

'I'm bored,' yelled Jacinta.

'Get your books and toys out of your bag. There's bound to be something interesting there.'

Jacinta got everything out of her holiday bag, and there at the bottom was the broken music box. She got back into bed with the music box and gave it a shake, as if that might bring the music back. The mermaid's shell made a little clunk inside. She opened the lid and there was just the tired little scratching sound of the broken music.

And then a seagull called in the distance and got closer and suddenly swooped right over the top of Jacinta's head, right through her bedroom, and more seagulls were calling now and instead of a square ceiling with corners there was a lovely high blue sky, just full of seagulls. A light, salty breeze was rising out of the music box and with it came the sound of the sea; swoosh, swoosh; waves were gently breaking all around Jacinta's bed, leaving sand on the duvet and sea shells on her pillow.

In among all the seaside sounds was music, just a few notes at first, and then more, until Jacinta could hear it clearly.

Someone, somewhere, was singing. They were singing the lost music from the broken music box.

'It's my mermaid! She's found my lost music. She's keeping it safe for me,' Jacinta said, and then she sneezed again.

When she closed the lid of the music box everything vanished as if it had never been there. Just as well, Jacinta thought. Mum would be cross about having the sea in my bedroom. She'd fuss about the carpet getting wet, and suppose I got washed away!

But none of that happened. Jacinta kept the sea and the lost music in her magic box, right until next summer, and let them out of the box just whenever she wanted.

Famous Seamus and the Ghosts of Football

STORY BY MALACHY DOYLE

ILLUSTRATED BY JOHN SHORT

THAT'S me in the picture. Famous Seamus! I suppose you're thinking I'm a bit young to be famous, but wait till you hear my story and maybe you'll change your mind.

And that old fellow next to me, the one with the beard, that's my granda. Not half as brave as me, but he's a good laugh, my granda. And he's always ready and willing to join me in my favourite pastime – going for long walks in the middle of the night.

Well, one time me and him were up in the hills by Slieve Gullion, camping. We were just settling down, all cosy-warm in our sleeping bags, when a dark shape appeared in the doorway.

'Who's that?' said my granda.

'Ah, it's nothing but a poor old sheep, coming in from the cold,' said I.

I can see in the dark, see. Didn't I tell you?

Then in walked another sheep. Followed by another. And another.

'There'll be no sleep here tonight,' said Granda.

So up we got and out we went. I led him through the pitch dark, till we came to a farmhouse.

'Is anyone in?' I cried, banging on the door.

It creaked open at last, and a craggy face appeared. It was an old fellow, older than my granda, even.

'Come on in out of the howling wind,' he said. 'Pull up a chair, the both of you, and I'll make us a nice pot of tea.'

'So what two things do you like most in the world?' said the farmer, sitting by the fire.

'Soccer and ghosts,' said I, quick as a flash.

'Soccer and ghosts!' said he. 'Well, there's a strange thing! Did you see that big castle up on the hill?'

'Too dark,' said my granda.

'Did you hear anything, then?'

'Too windy.'

'Well that's where you ought to be, young man, if it's ghosts and soccer you're after,' said the farmer.

'How do you mean?' said I.

'That old castle's full of ghosts!' said he. 'Ghosts playing football! Every night, for the last I-don't-know-how-long, there's never a wink of sleep to be had in this here house what with all the noise coming from up on that there hill. Kicking a ball up and down the Great Hall of Narrow Water Castle all night, they are. Echoes, it does, down the hill, up the stairs, and into my poor tired ears.'

I looked at my granda, and he looked away.

'Ah, come on, Granda,' said I. 'We'll just take a wee look. See if we can get those old ghosts to play a bit quieter.'

So up I got and out I went, and Granda had no choice but to follow me.

Trudging through the pitch dark night, we were, when, 'Listen!' I said.

But there was nothing to hear but the hooting of owls.

Then, 'Listen!' I said, but there was nothing to hear but the baaing of sheep from inside our tent.

Then, 'Listen!' I said, and there it was. The thumping and bashing, banging and yelling of ghosts. Ghosts playing football!

'I'm away back down to the old farmer,' said my granda.

'No, you're not,' said I, hanging onto him.

So in we went, through the creaky old door that looked like it hadn't been opened in a hundred years, down the cobwebby corridor and into the Great Hall of Narrow Water Castle.

And there before our eyes was the strangest sight you've ever seen. Eleven red and white ghosts kicking a battered

old football around the room.

And each one of them dressed in the full 1948 United kit, baggy shorts and all.

'Frankie!' yelled my granda, and he ran over to the one with the captain's armband on, grabbed his hand, and started pumping it up and down.

'Frankie Molloy, my lifelong hero! Sure, everyone thought you had died years ago!'

'I did,' said the ghost, grumpily. 'But they won't let me rest in peace. I have to go on playing this stupid game till someone blows the final whistle.'

I'd never heard of Frankie Molloy, to tell you the truth, but if Granda thought he was great then that was good enough for me, so I reached down into the deep, deep pockets of my long, long overcoat and pulled out my autograph book. I always carry it with me on my night-time rambles – you never know who you might meet.

Frankie kicked the ball to my granda, who passed it to me, and I dribbled it down the hall, round Danny Carr, through Tony Harvey's legs, and slammed it past the goalie, Safehands O'Sullivan.

'Blimey, Seamus,' said my granda. 'That's the best goal I've ever seen you score. And against United, too!'

Frankie stopped the game and came up to me.

'Not bad, Seamus,' he said. 'We could have done with you in the 1948 final.'

'You're right, Frankie,' said Granda, sadly. 'Wasn't I there at Windsor Park with my very own granda cheering you on? One–nil to the Rovers – sure it nearly broke my heart. I can still hear the sound of the final whistle, ringing in my ears.'

'But you can't!' said Frankie. 'That's the whole point – the ref never blew the final whistle! It was in his mouth, and he was looking for his watch, when big Buster McBurnie of the Rovers bashed into him. The ref swallowed the whistle, someone in the crowd blew one of theirs, and everyone thought we'd lost.'

'So the game's not over yet?' said Granda. 'There's still a chance to win the Cup?'

'Yes,' said Frankie. 'That's why we're here, in this freezing old castle, kicking a ball round, us downstairs and the Rovers up, till some sort of ref comes along and lets us finish the match.'

'Have no fear,' I cried, thinking fast. 'Seamus is here!'

And I reached down into the deep, deep pocket of my long, long overcoat. For guess what else I always carry with me on my night-time rambles. A whistle! In case I get lost. I pulled it out and gave a great blast.

WHEEEEEEE!

Suddenly there was a terrific clatter of boots on the staircase, and in rushed another eleven baggy footballers.

'Game on!' cried my granda, grabbing the whistle from my lips. 'It's one–nil to the Rovers, and there's two minutes left!'

The twenty-two ghosts ran around like mad things, chasing the ball up and down the Great Hall, until . . .

'Aaargh!' Danny Carr fell in a heap.

'It's cramp!' he cried, rubbing his leg. 'You'll have to take me off, Captain.'

'But I can't,' said Frankie, looking desperately round the room. 'We haven't any substitutes.'

And then his ghostly eyes fell upon me.

'Oh yes we have . . .' he said. 'Seamus, the super sub! You're on, boy!'

So Danny tore off his kit, I threw it on, and there I was, centre forward for United in the dying moments of the 1948 final! A goal down and less than two minutes to play.

WHEEEEE! went my granda, and the ball came flying towards me. I chested it down, dummied the Rovers left back and slammed it past the keeper. One all!

WHEEEEEE! went my granda again, checking his watch. The centre forward kicked off from the spot, passed it to Buster McBurnie and he came flying towards me.

He's massive, Buster McBurnie! More like a steamroller than a footballer. No one tackles him and survives to tell the tale. He'll flatten me, I thought. I'll be the one who'll have to rest in peace. So I was all set to dodge out of his way at the last moment, when that old streak of bravery that always gets me in so much trouble took over. I stuck out my leg and tried to roll the ball off his foot. And it worked!

'Run, Frankie!' I yelled, and the captain took off, down the left wing. I floated the ball over to him and raced on towards goal, with Buster puffing away behind me like a steam train. Frankie did a beautiful first-time overhead pass, straight to my head, and I whacked it with all my might into the top right-hand corner.

WHEEEEE! went my granda, and the game was over. Two–one to United!

'We've done it at last! We've won the Cup!' cried Frankie, hoisting me onto his shoulders.

'Three cheers for Famous Seamus!' he yelled, taking me on a lap of honour round the room.

Everyone cheered, even the Rovers, who were just glad to finish the game at last. My granda joined in, though he had to do it quietly, of course, because he was the referee.

And one by one, as the ghostly footballers came up to shake my hand, they disappeared into thin air! Never to be seen again! And all there was left in the Great Hall of Narrow Water Castle was me, my granda, and the very football I am holding in my hands before you!

So now do you see why I'm famous?

The Secret Stone

STORY BY MARITA CONLON-MCKENNA

ILLUSTRATED BY BRIAN GALLAGHER

ISOBEL watched the shimmering blue of the ocean below her change as the huge airplane began its landing descent. Her dad squeezed her hand.

'Isn't it good to be going home, Isobel, back home to Ireland. You'll see my new apartment, and I can't wait to take you down the country to meet your granny and cousins and show you where I grew up.'

Isobel said nothing, nothing at all, but watched the pattern of green fields and hedges and curving roads getting bigger and bigger. Home wasn't here; it was back in New York where her mommy was, not this strange new country where her dad was going to live and work.

Isobel fixed the straps of her backpack across her shoulders as her dad collected the luggage and told her all about his new home and the things they'd do together during her summer stay.

Dad's new apartment was big and modern, a lot bigger than she had imagined and her dad proudly showed her all around it.

Isobel said nothing and just stared at the blank white walls and wooden floors as he opened another door.

'This is your room, Isobel pet. Whenever you come to visit me, this is your room!

'We can paint it pink or yellow or whatever you want! Decorate it with cats or dogs, dolphins or stars, just any way you'd like it!'

Isobel closed her lips tight, refusing to answer him, not even saying a word.

'Come on, Isobel! Tell me what you think. Say something!' begged her dad.

Outside on the balcony he pointed out the quays and the winding river Liffey, which flowed through Dublin city. Isobel watched the crowds of busy people below rushing around, crossing back and forwards on the bridges, and thought of her mom back home in America.

Mom and Dad had told her on a Sunday when she'd come home from swimming, her hair still wet, the smell of chlorine on her skin. They told her how much they both loved and cared for her, but it was just that they had stopped loving each other.

Her mom and dad explained that it was far better for everyone, while they were still friends, to not live together any more and in time, like lots of other people, get a divorce. Isobel had sat there, totally still, listening, watching them, refusing to say a word about it, wrapping the silence around her like a warm blanket.

In Dublin her dad showed her all over the city. He bought her a blue rain jacket, a pair of yellow boots and an umbrella just in case it rained. They ate pizza and pancakes and fat Irish sausages that sizzled in the pan. Her dad was happier than she'd seen him in a long, long time.

Two days later they drove to the country to see her granny and meet the cousins, her dad singing in the car.

'You'll love it,' said her dad. 'There was always a bit of magic about the place.'

The old farmhouse in Sligo had a black tiled roof and whitewashed walls. A brown collie dog barked and jumped on her the very minute she stepped out of the car, Granny telling it to hush up and scooping her up in her arms for a hug and a kiss, tears filling her eyes when she saw Dad.

Hungry, Isobel ate two plates of her granny's stew in the kitchen as Granny told her all about the times when Dad was a boy.

Dad and Granny showed her the barn and the hen house and the top field where the cows grazed and the little river near the oak wood. Isobel helped her granny to feed the hens and patted the farm cat. She silently counted out the cabbages that were growing in a row near the back door.

Later, her uncles and aunts and cousins all arrived tumbling in the door, shouting and laughing and all excited to meet her. Isobel politely shook their hands. She had ten cousins, who all pushed and shoved and tried to get her attention. Isobel did her best to remember all the Irish-sounding names as her granny fetched hot, buttery scones and raspberry jam and a big apple tart with thick cream. Isobel could feel them all looking at her but still wouldn't say a word.

'She's as quiet as a mouse!' joked her Uncle Sean and Isobel wished that she could scamper and hide away like a real little mouse.

Her cousins Mikey and Niall sang two songs and her cousin Niamh did an Irish jig but when they asked Isobel to sing or say a poem she just shook her head.

Every day they came, the cousins with their smiling faces, Isobel sat quietly and listened to their jokes and stories, never saying a word.

'Why won't Isobel talk to us?' asked little Liam, her four-year-old cousin.

Isobel tried not to cry when they all stared at her.

'You lot talk far too much,' said her granny kindly. 'Now away out and play in the fresh air!'

The next night, when Isobel was lying in bed trying not to feel sad and lonesome, her granny came into the room and called her.

'Isobel pet, put on your shoes, and something warm, it's a beautiful night out and we should be up and enjoying it!'

Isobel had no slippers, so she shoved her feet into her new yellow boots and pulled on the big thick sweater her granny had knitted for her during the winter over her nightdress.

The two of them slipped outside. The clear, starry night was cold and Isobel walked alongside her grandmother, trying not to stumble in the dark.

'There's magic in the air on a night like this, Isobel, can you feel it!'

Isobel nodded.

'Your grandfather and I loved to walk out across our fields on such a night. This farm is such a special place.'

The moonlight lit up the spiky bushes and tall trees, making everything look strange and different.

'Here we are!' whispered her granny, coming to a halt outside the low field. 'This is it!'

Isobel stared and stared, unsure of what she was meant to be looking at.

'Can't you see it!' urged her grandmother softly.

Isobel looked all around and about her but she couldn't see a thing, just the grass and the bushes and the way the ground ran together, making some sort of circle.

'It's a fairy ring,' murmured her granny. 'An enchanted place that belongs to the "Sidhe" – the little people.'

Isobel gasped. Looking at it now in the moonlight, she could see it clearly, the huge broad band of the ring running across the sloping field.

'For hundreds of years, maybe more, the little people have lived here, prospered, the fairy ring undisturbed.

Your grandfather and his father would never allow anyone or anything to harm such a spot or anger them.'

Isobel stood transfixed, wondering what her granny was trying to tell her.

'When your grandfather died, it was as much as I could do to keep the farm going. My heart wasn't in it. All I wanted to do was to roll up in the bed and never go out of the house again. The farm here could have gone to ruin for all I cared. But you know the strangest thing – we had the best laying hens in the district, our cows gave the creamiest milk and our vegetables grew big and strong . . . the Sidhe did it.'

Isobel looked wide-eyed at her grandmother.

'It can only have been them. The little people helped me when I needed it most. Perhaps they could help you too. If you look long and hard you might be lucky enough to see them, Isobel, but even if you don't, they'll see you.'

Isobel looked around the fairy ring, nervous, wondering if they were watching her.

'See that stone in the middle?' said Granny.

Isobel nodded.

'That's the famous Sweeney stone.'

Isobel had never ever heard of the stone.

'It's the very tip of their secret castle, which stretches for miles underground.'

To Isobel it looked like a big piece of old grey rock that stuck up from the ground, nothing special at all.

'Your daddy kissed it when he was a boy, and your Uncle Sean and Auntie Liz and all the family, your cousins Mikey and Niamh and all the rest of them, and I was just wondering if you'd like to follow on the Sweeney family tradition and kiss the stone too.'

Isobel shook her head, unsure.

'Maybe you need a little bit of magic,' whispered her granny softly.

As they gently entered the fairy ring, Isobel, scared, imagined hundreds of eyes watching her.

'Kneel down there on the grass, pet,' her granny urged,

'and don't touch the stone with your hands. Just place your lips against it.'

In the silence of the night with the stars shining down on her, Isobel believed, and kneeling down on the damp dewy grass she touched her lips to the cold rough stone, which jutted up from the earth. Her mouth seemed to cling to it, sticking to it for a few seconds before she stood up. She shivered in the night air.

'Come, Isobel, it's time to get back,' smiled her grandmother, putting her arms gently around her.

The early morning sun came in the bedroom window and tickled along the blue, woollen blanket, waking Isobel. The cat was cleaning its paws and watching her from the rug on the floor.

'Good morning, Trixie! Good morning!' cried Isobel.

The words seemed to bubble up from inside her and spill out into the sunshine.

She talked to the hens as she fed them and to the new calf in the barn and Lucky, the brown collie dog, who wagged his tail and licked her face with excitement. She talked to her granny, who was thrilled and hugged her and told her to remember the stone was a family secret. And she talked to her dad, who pulled her into his arms and buried his face in her hair.

The rest of the Irish holiday passed far too quickly and before she knew it Isobel had to say goodbye to her granny and her cousins and the farm in Sligo. Her dad and herself were staying a night in Dublin before she was to fly back home.

'I can't wait to see Mom again,' smiled Isobel, bursting with news and so many things to tell.

Her dad looked sad and quiet as she packed her bag. He checked her passport and ticket, neither of them wanting to say goodbye. They were just about to leave when Isobel remembered something and ran back into the bedroom of the apartment and took some things from her bag. She hung her shiny raincoat in the empty wardrobe and placed her umbrella and her yellow boots on the shelf, all ready for the next time she came back to see her dad and visit Ireland and the secret stone.

Reverse Flannery

POEM BY PAUL MULDOON

ILLUSTRATED BY NIAMH SHARKEY

WHEN he felt not a head but the ball of a foot
Doctor Grimley turned to a nurse:
'My lunch with Ignatius Herring's gone kaput.
For this kid is stuck in reverse.'

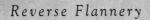

Not only did Mrs Pam Flannery come to
momentarily but she came
(as she drifted in and out of the flitter-flew
of consciousness), upon a name.

For, until then, her daughter was meant to be dubbed
Fionnuala or Florence or Fay,
the daughter who, from the hour of her birth, had rubbed
everybody up the wrong way.

Reverse was herself a little bent out of shape
in the process of being born
when Doctor Grimley's forceps caught her by the nape,
leaving a scar like a moon's horn.

She could have been little more than eighteen months old
when she got into hot water
for arguing that the bath was much, much too cold
for Mrs Dannery's flaughter.

It may have been because of her permanent frown
that people began to suppose
that she was always a little mouth in the down,
her joint a little out of nose.

By the time Reverse was eight or nine years of age
she was a creature of habits
such as warring a wage and comebacking a stage
and pulling hats out of rabbits.

She loved sago for starters, sausages for sweet,
Knockman's Post and Thimble the Hunt.
How could anyone manage to look quite so neat
while wearing her frock back to front?

Reverse Flannery

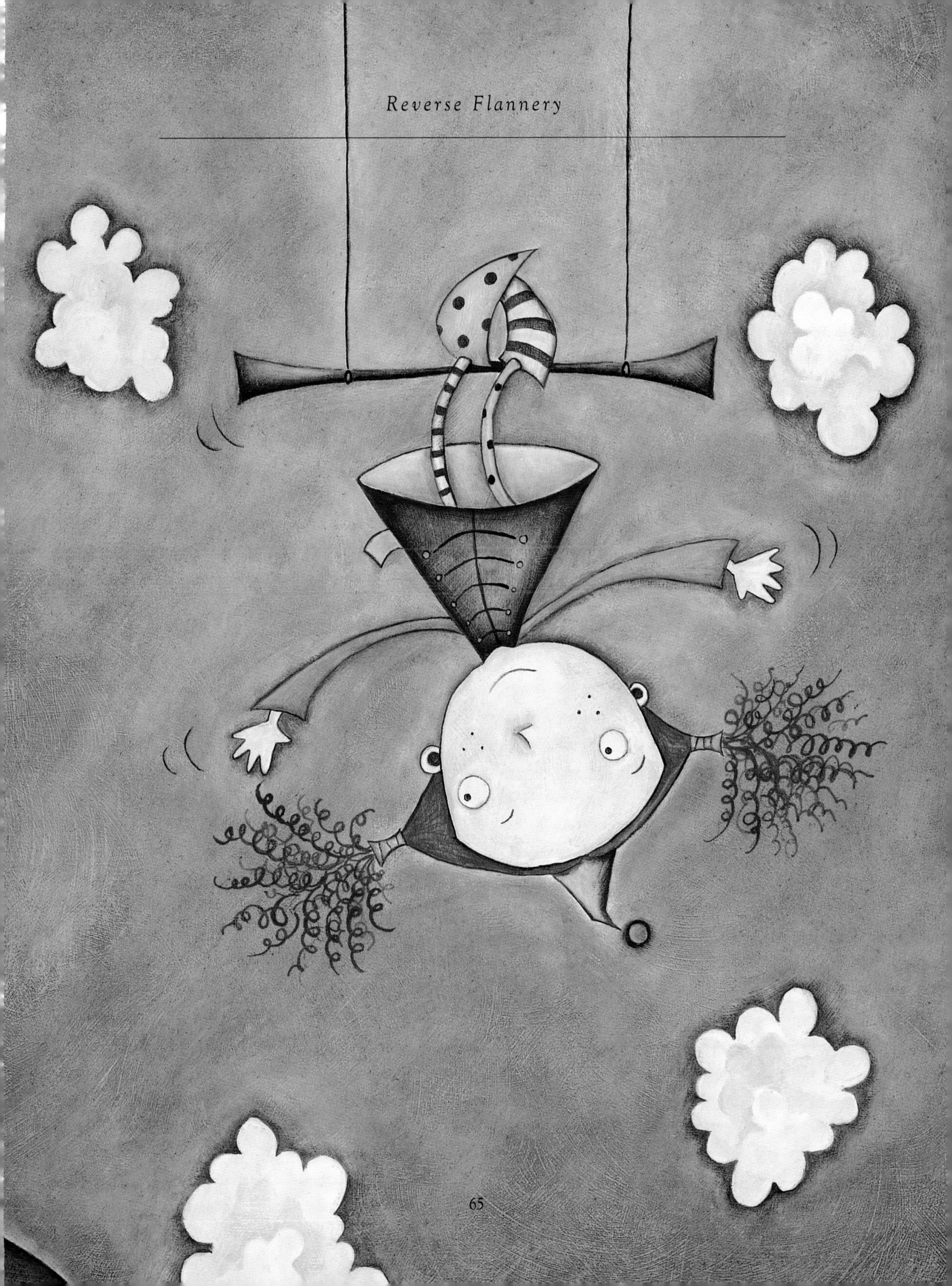

Her socks were always outside in, or inside out,
her cap always topsy-turvy.
Sam Flannery gave her a daily sip of stout
to ward off sore throats and scurvy.

Down Under

That went only so far to explain why her shoes
were always on opposite feet,
or why Reverse Flannery herself flitter-flew
by the pants – the *pants* – of her seat.

She'd list *The Three Little Wolves and the Big Bad Pig*,
Peter Rabbit's *Beatrix Potter*,
Matilda's *Roald Dahl*, The Snowman's *Raymond Briggs*,
as books she'd read, in her jotter.

That went only so far to explain why Reverse
was so disliked by one and all.
Her schoolmates made fun of how she would lip her purse.
Her parents wouldn't take her calls.

That was partly because, when Reverse sat an exam,
she somehow tended to unlearn
all she knew, and when the results reached Pam and Sam
things often took an ugly turn.

It got so bad that, as she walked through town one day
and saw an ad for 'Down Under'
in a bucket shop, Reverse was, as she would say,
boundspelled, smackgobbed and struckthunder.

And she resolved, over a cup of lukewarm spit
in the back of the Blue Dahlia
that she would jaw her set, take the mouth in her bit,
and run away to Australia.

She went home and, instead of a spotted hankie,
borrowed one of her mother's scarves,
in which she wrapped bread, steak, a fishhook, a manky
old map of Sydney's docks and wharves,

plus a red swimming suit trimmed with off-white, or grey –
quite a fetching little number
she planned to wear to Bondi Beach on Christmas Day
(which falls, of course, in high summer).

As Reverse was making her way down the back stairs
she heard her dad sniff and snort,
'You get in here this minute, Miss Putting-on-Airs,
and explain this latest report.'

It came from her new teacher, Ignatius Herring
(that old friend of Doctor Grimley),
who wrote: 'Reverse Flannery has an unerring
eye for a striking simile,

while her ear for a most inventive turn of phrase
is so very, very refined
that I've nothing to offer but the highest praise
for her quite original mind.'

Sam Flannery's sniffs and snorts proved to have been fake.
Now he began to quiver-quake
with laughter so profound the house began to shake.
When she'd realized her mistake,

Reverse and her mum and dad were able to make
up over a dinner of bread, steak,
and a slice of the pineapple upside-down cake
Pam had come home early to bake.

Since then, Reverse has always been top of her class,
scoring ninety-nine or higher
in every test she's sat, so managing to pass,
she says, 'with colouring fliers'.

As Reverse moves on to Saint Thomas of the Doubt's
Grammar School in the Antrim Hills,
Ignatius Herring is already looking out
for someone who might shoe her fills.

The Seal That Did Not Forget

STORY BY JAMES RIORDAN

ILLUSTRATED BY JON BERKELEY

'HUSH and listen to the wind. Do you hear a baby's cry?'

'I do that,' said Fergal.

'And I,' cried little Una.

'That's the grey seal calling me from the bay.'

The children laughed. Grandad Dinny O'Rourke was always pulling their legs.

'And why should a seal be calling you?' asked Una.

'Whist now. Listen to my tale an' you'll understand.'

They were sitting on the rocks overlooking Bantry Bay. It was a still summer's evening: the weary sun was glistening on a gently rippling sea.

''Tis a while back, when I was a young man. Each day I'd go out at dawn to gather periwinkles in the sand. That morning, as I recall, the sea had the blush of spring upon it, all bright and rosy. I was wading in rocky pools at the water's edge when I caught a moaning on the breeze. It was scary, all full of pain. Though I glanced about, I saw nothing but lapping waves.

'Then, all at once, I spotted a big grey seal behind some rocks, its head above the waves. It was staring wide-eyed into the pool. Even as I came near, it never dived into the sea, nor took its eyes off the pool.

'I waded through the swell and suddenly saw that it was a mother seal with two young pups. They were sheltering in one corner of the pool. The pups must have been just born, for they were groping blindly for her teats.

'What a stroke of luck, I think. Those baby seals will make fine soft gloves.

'And I splashed towards the pool. In panic, the mother seal swiftly rowed herself over the rock into the sea. But there was no escape for her pups. I grabbed them both and would have hurried home had not an odd sound stopped me dead.

'The mother seal was rolling over and over in the water, slapping the sea with her fins. Then she hauled herself onto the rock and looked straight into my face. Her big brown eyes gave me such a begging look they would have melted a heart of stone. But not me. Oh no! I was a hard-hearted devil in those days.

'With the pair of pups under my arms, I took a step towards the shore. Then a strange noise came from behind me. The mother gave a groan so human it made me look round.

'She was lying on her side, head upon the rock. And I saw tears brimming in her eyes and rolling down her face. If seals could speak I swear she was saying, "Sir, I beg of you, take pity and spare my pups."

'That was more than I could bear.

'I bent down and gently laid the pups upon the rock. At once she took them in her fins and clasped them to her breast – just like any mother with her young. And she gave me such a grateful look.

'Well, as I told you, I was but a slip of a lad then. Soon I married and went to live up Dingle way. Many years passed before I returned to Bantry. One day I went fishing in the bay. Sure I was the luckiest fisher that ever lived. The fish were biting so well. I swear it was the grey seal's doing. And now she sits on the rock in Bantry Bay, singing to me. The seal that did not forget.'

Both children laughed at the tall story.

'Get away with you, Grandad,' cried Fergal. 'You're making it up. Seals don't cry.'

'And they can't sing,' added Una with a grin.

Grandad O'Rourke just smiled to himself.

A few days later the children were alone upon the shore. They were searching the rocky pools for shiny stones and sea-shells to take back to school. So busy were they that they quite forgot about the tide.

When at last they turned to go, they cried out in alarm. Between them and the shore the sea was deep enough to cover their heads. Although they screamed and yelled, they were too far out for anyone to hear.

The water rose and rose, came up to their knees, their waist, their chest. Soon it came up to little Una's chin. Even if they could swim, they would never have strength to reach the shore.

There seemed no hope of being saved.

Yet, all at once, a wave knocked them off their feet and bore them through the sea towards the beach. It held up their heads and only let them go when their feet touched the sand.

Thankfully, they waded ashore.

Looking round, they were amazed to see two seals swimming out to sea.

When they told Grandad O'Rourke of their adventure, he was full of fear. How close they'd come to drowning! But, later, as all three sat holding hands on the rocks, he suddenly shouted out, 'God bless the seal that did not forget!'

Wherever

STORY BY KATE THOMPSON

ILLUSTRATED BY HAMILTON SLOAN

WHEREVER there are fairies, there's sure to be music. I don't remember who it was that told me that, but I know I believed it, and for the whole of that day out in the countryside I had my ears open, listening.

We climbed up to the fort at the top of the hill. The walls were high and green, and the blackthorn bushes were still standing sentry but there was nobody dancing there. The only sound was the wind. The magicians who had built the place were gone.

We crawled down into the long halls beneath the hill, and muddied our bellies and our knees. The candle-light showed us the work of their long-ago hands, but the shadows it cast were all ours. The little people who had lived here, banished from Ireland's forests and fields, had taken their gold and left their homes silent and dark.

We went into the woods and stood in their dappled

green light. There were hazel-cup heaps and twisty little paths and brambly tunnels and dark little doorways, but it wasn't the fairy folk who had made them. It was foxes and badgers and squirrels and mice.

'They've gone, haven't they?' I asked Dad.

'Who?'

'The Good People. They've gone back where they came from. Back to Tir na n'Og.'

Dad thought about that for a long time. Then he said, 'Some of them have gone, perhaps. But not all of them.'

We watched a brown hare cross over a long meadow.

'That might be one of them,' said Dad. 'And the raven that we saw passing over the fort.'

I didn't think so, though, and Dad knew it. He gave me a funny little secret smile. 'I'm surprised at you,' he said. 'I would have thought that you knew exactly where they are.'

'Why?'

We walked back towards the car. 'Well,' said Dad. 'If you were one of the fairy folk, and if you wanted to keep your spirit alive among the people who loved you, what would you become?'

All the way back in the car I racked my brains, but I couldn't come up with the answer.

I suppose all that walking must have tired me out. I know I didn't mean to go to sleep. I didn't even get into my pyjamas. I just lay down on the bed, just for a minute, to think about that question that Dad had asked. I went through everything I knew about the fairies. As far as I could remember, they had never come among people much at all. They had always stayed apart, living in their own world, just touching the edges of ours from time to time. But there was one thing we shared with them, a great love that the people and the fairies shared. What was it?

They woke me with their answer. The house was full of them, full of their dancing and their laughter and their wild, mischievous spirit. I sat up in bed. Of course I knew where they lived. I had always known.

Downstairs in the kitchen, my parents were playing their fiddles. There were other musicians there as well; I could hear a flute and a concertina. Beside my bed, my whistle was glowing in the dark, pleading with me to play it.

I reached out for it and ran downstairs.

The kitchen was warm and soft with the fairies' magic light. I hadn't been so far wrong, after all. Just got the words back to front. Where else could they be, after all, if not in the instruments they brought into our lives and the music they taught us to play?

Dad winked at me and led straight off into a tune that I knew. The whistle trembled beneath my fingers like a living thing.

Wherever there is music, there are sure to be fairies.

The
Princess
and the
Rooster

STORY BY CARLO GÉBLER

ILLUSTRATED BY PAULINE BEWICK

CONOR, the youngest son of the king of Sligo, was sailing to Rome when his ship sank in a storm. He was washed ashore on an island ruled by an old witch.

'You're my slave now,' she said and put him to work at once. 'A magic eel lives under these waters. Catch it and bring it to me. I want its powers.'

It took Conor three long months to hook that magic eel, and when he did he decided to keep it for himself. He gulped it down with one big swallow.

'Enjoy that?' screeched a passing seagull and without thinking Conor called back, 'Yes.' And then he knew. Whoever ate the eel was able to speak the languages of the animals.

The next morning Conor began speaking to the witch's pet dog. The witch overheard and knew all. 'You ate the magic eel,' she shrieked. And she turned Conor into a rooster right then and there. 'Now I'm going to eat you,' she said.

As she lunged at him, Conor flapped his wings, rose into the sky and set off back to Ireland.

He flew for many days and nights and landed in the garden of the king of Kerry, exhausted. The king, a good and fair king called Ciaran, was widowed and lived with his only child, the eighteen-year-old Princess Veronica. When the king, who loved all animals, spotted the rooster he caught him and placed him in a beautiful painted roost. Then he called his daughter over to see.

'Cock-a-doodle-do. Please release me,' cried Conor. 'I was on my way home.' The king and his daughter stepped back in surprise for they had never heard an animal talk.

The king was set to release him when Veronica begged him to let her keep the rooster. And the king, who could never refuse his daughter anything, said, 'You must stay, Rooster. Each dawn you will crow and wake all the inhabitants of Kerry, and during the day you will be my daughter's companion.'

But the king had another, secret, reason for keeping the rooster. Later, in private, he told the rooster, 'Beyond the walled garden stalks a huge ogre who rules the kingdom of darkness. Every night you will act as lookout. Your crowing will warn the palace infantry of his approach. Veronica must never know of this danger.'

The rooster settled easily into his new home and his new routine. And before long he and Veronica were inseparable. She sang to him and he read to her, and together they played in the palace gardens. And soon Conor was in love with her, for although he was a rooster now he had once been a man.

Time passed and one summer's morning, the princess rushed into the king's bedroom. 'Last night I dreamt a giant was stamping around the garden wall, trying to get in.'

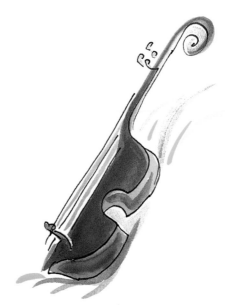

The king tried to hide his concern and fetched a fiddle and bow from the wardrobe. 'This is a special fiddle,' he said, 'that will play at the clap of a hand. If a nightmare wakes you, music from this will lull you back to sleep.'

The next morning Veronica appeared at her father's bedroom once again. 'I dreamt of the giant last night,' she said. 'I woke and the music didn't put me to sleep.'

The king went to the wardrobe and this time took out a rug. 'One hand clap and this rug will unravel, two hand claps it will re-weave itself. Watching this should put you back to sleep,' he said, trying to soothe his daughter.

On the third morning Veronica ran to the king's bedroom. 'I dreamt of the giant last night. When I woke I played with the rug but I still couldn't sleep.'

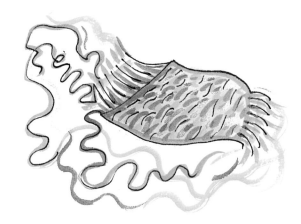

The king, who was now very upset, went to his wardrobe and removed a needle. 'At the clap of a hand the needle will thread itself and sew as directed. Needlework will help you get back to sleep.' And Veronica and the king both hoped this would do the trick.

That very afternoon Conor and Veronica lay in hammocks in the orchard in the hot sun. For fun, Veronica

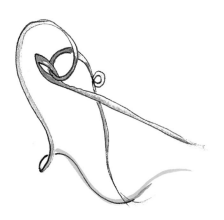

tipped the rooster out of his. She did not see the axe left by a careless gardener lying in the long grass below. The laughing rooster fell with his mouth open. The blade cut off his tongue, and his blood spilt on the grass.

The princess screamed for help.

A huge figure leapt over the wall and Veronica stared up in horror. Conor realized instantly it was the ogre. He knew he must warn Veronica but how, when he could not speak?

'Can you put his tongue back?' she pleaded.

'Yes, but in return the rooster must work for me every day from midnight until morning for as long as he lives.'

Conor flapped his wings frantically as a warning against the ogre's proposal, but Veronica took this as a sign of pain.

'And you will return him by dawn?' pleaded Veronica.

'Agreed,' bellowed the ogre. 'Now fetch me your needle and thread and something to put the rooster to sleep.'

Veronica fetched the special presents her father had given her and returned. She clapped her hands, the fiddle played, and Conor fell asleep.

Veronica clapped again and the carpet unravelled.

She clapped a third time and the needle threaded a strand from the carpet through its eye.

The ogre nodded. 'Very good,' he said. 'I'll take over now.'

Then the ogre placed Conor's tongue back in his mouth and shouted, 'Sew.'

The needle darted forward and set to work.

The job was done, the music stopped and Conor opened his eyes.

Then the ogre reached in his pocket for a handful of dust, blew it into Veronica's eyes and she went to sleep.

'She will remember nothing,' he said. 'Rooster, I will see you tonight.' The ogre vaulted the wall and was gone.

Veronica opened her eyes. Where the rooster's blood had splashed, small red flowers had sprung up. 'Did these grow while I was asleep?' she murmured, for she remembered nothing.

That night, the ogre fetched Conor and brought him to a massive set of gates in the middle of darkness. 'Here,' he said, handing Conor a sword, a shield and a helmet. 'Only the dead may pass through these gates. You must chase away the living. They often come and try to get the dead back. You must stop them.'

And night after night, Conor stood at the gates and every dawn he returned to his roost. His crowing got weaker and weaker. Finally, he climbed on his perch one morning and saw the sun rising but when he opened his beak nothing came out. Watching the dead had driven the joy from his heart and robbed him of his power to crow.

The town woke late that day and no one could understand the rooster's silence.

'Why didn't you crow this morning?' asked Veronica.

How could he tell her of the nightly pain he suffered, when it was she who had agreed he become the ogre's slave?

After that, Conor's heart grew colder and colder. He no longer read to Veronica, she no longer sang to him and they no longer played together in the garden. They were friends no more.

One night, years later, when Conor was standing guard, who should appear but the old king, Ciaran. Conor, with his heart of flint, no longer felt anything for the dead, but on seeing the king as he passed through the gates, pity welled up in him.

A tear splashed from each eye. These were caught by the wind, carried to the palace and dropped onto the eyelids of the sleeping princess. They trickled into her eyes and dissolved the ogre's dust. Suddenly she could remember everything.

Later that same night she saw her father in a dream and called out, 'How can I free Conor from the agreement I made?'

'Pick the red flowers,' he said, 'that grow in the orchard. While the fiddle plays have the needle sew them into a crown using thread from the carpet. Put the crown on Conor's head and he will be free.'

As dawn broke Veronica made the crown. Then she ran to the roost.

The rooster was back from the gates and was fast asleep. She gently placed the crown on his head and then she left.

Later, when Conor woke, he opened his mouth and cried, 'Cock-a-doodle-doo,' without thinking. It was the first time he had crowed in years.

Veronica, hearing this, ran back to the roost. When she got there she found not a bird but a man.

For it was not only the ogre's power that was broken but the witch's too.

Conor was now just as he was the day the witch had transformed him – a man who could speak the language of the animals.

He told Veronica his strange story. They became friends once more, reading, singing and playing together in the palace gardens, and seven days later they were married.

The ogre still roamed beyond the garden walls, but never again set foot inside the palace.

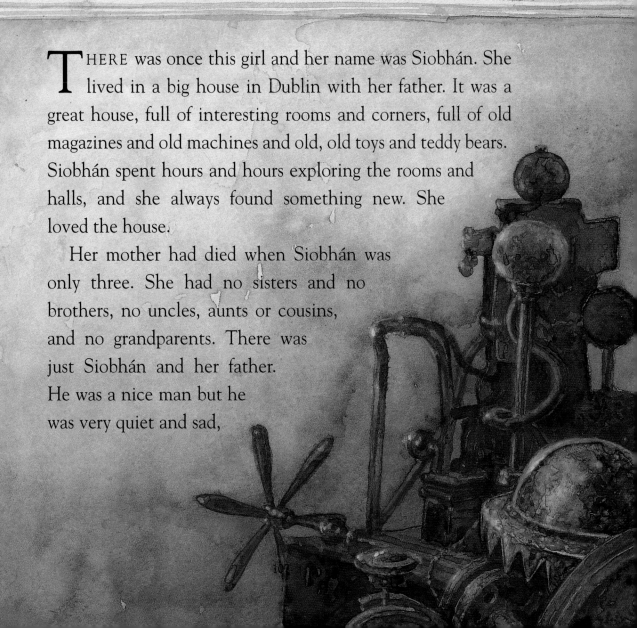

Her Mother's Face

STORY BY RODDY DOYLE

ILLUSTRATED BY P. J. LYNCH

T HERE was once this girl and her name was Siobhán. She lived in a big house in Dublin with her father. It was a great house, full of interesting rooms and corners, full of old magazines and old machines and old, old toys and teddy bears. Siobhán spent hours and hours exploring the rooms and halls, and she always found something new. She loved the house.

Her mother had died when Siobhán was only three. She had no sisters and no brothers, no uncles, aunts or cousins, and no grandparents. There was just Siobhán and her father. He was a nice man but he was very quiet and sad, and he kept himself to himself. He read to Siobhán sometimes. He brought her home a new book every Friday. He smiled whenever he saw her looking at him but he never spoke to her about her mother. In fact, nobody ever spoke to Siobhán about her mother.

Siobhán was ten now and she could not remember her mother's face. She had searched every corner of the house. She found her mother's old books and a scarf and a pair of mad green shoes, but she never found a photograph.

Siobhán could remember her mother's hands. Her hands combing Siobhán's hair, her hands peeling an apple, holding the steering wheel, pulling up Siobhán's sock, and her hands on her lap when Siobhán was brought into the dark room to say goodbye to her. When Siobhán closed her eyes, she could see her mother's hands doing these things and other things but, no matter how hard she tried or how long she kept her eyes closed, she couldn't see her mother's face.

She could remember her mother's voice. And she could remember some words.

'Cat and spuds for dinner, Siobhán. How does that sound?'

'Yeuk.'

'Yeuk cat? Or yeuk spuds?'

'Yeuk cat.'

'OK. We'll have chicken instead.'

And she could remember her mother singing 'Did you ever shove your granny off the bus?' She could hear her mother but she could never see her face.

The empty space where her mother's face should have been was like a pain, a giant unhappiness, that Siobhán carried with her everywhere. When she saw other mothers hugging their children, or buttoning their coats, and even when she saw her friends' mothers giving out to her friends, the pain grew in her chest and pushed tears up to her eyes. And, as she got older, the pain got worse and worse because her mother seemed to be going further and further away.

Other children liked Siobhán. They liked sitting beside her in school. She never argued, and she never whinged or grabbed and broke things. She made them laugh. She would cross her eyes and say the things that adults love saying.

'Money doesn't grow on trees.'

'It's raining cats and dogs.'

'I have eyes in the back of my head.'

Her friends all knew that Siobhán's mother was dead but none of them knew how sad she was. She never told them and she never let them see.

When she tried
to talk to her father
about her mother, his
face would fill with
worry and sadness, and
she'd stop. He hugged her once and
said, 'Sorry.' They had a pizza and
watched telly together. It was nice,
but they didn't talk.

One day, Siobhán was sitting in
Saint Anne's Park, very near her
house. She sat under a huge chestnut
tree. She could remember her
mother's hands holding her up, high
enough to pull a conker from the
lowest branch. She could remember
her voice.

'The big one, the big one. Grab it.
Yesss!'

She could remember how it felt,
the hands squeezing through her
dress, the nice safe feeling, knowing
that she wouldn't fall.

She tried to remember turning, to smile at her mother, but she couldn't. This was what Siobhán was doing, trying to remember, when she heard a voice.

'Hello.'

Siobhán looked and saw a beautiful woman standing beside her. The woman sat beside Siobhán, on the grass. Most adults never did this because it was quite mucky and damp.

'You're sad, aren't you?' said the beautiful woman.

She had dark brown hair, like Siobhán's, and brown eyes. And she had a friendly smile and a lovely voice. Siobhán never spoke to strangers but this woman didn't seem like a stranger.

'Yes,' said Siobhán. 'I am sad. A bit.'

'Why?' said the woman.

And Siobhán told her. She told her everything. About her mother's death and her hands and about how she could never see her mother's face. And she cried as she spoke but she didn't mind. She just kept talking.

The woman listened and smiled.

'You know what you should do?' she said when Siobhán had finished talking.

'What?' said Siobhán.

The woman wiped Siobhán's eyes with the sleeve of her coat.

'You should look in the mirror,' said the woman.

'Why?' said Siobhán.

'Because then you'll see your mother,' said the woman. 'You'll see the way she looked when she was your age. And, as you get older, you'll see what your mother looked like when she was getting older.'

Then she kissed Siobhán, and hugged her. 'How's your daddy?' she said.

'He's fine,' said Siobhán. 'But he's very sad too.'

'Give him a message from me,' said the woman. 'Tell him . . .'

And she whispered the message into Siobhán's ear.

Siobhán laughed.

'Why?' she said.

'Just tell him and then he'll tell you,' said the woman.

And then she stood up.

'Goodbye, Siobhán,' said the woman. 'We'll meet again, I'm sure.'

She walked away, out of the park.

Siobhán went home and up to the bathroom and looked in the mirror. At first, all she could see was her own face. But she stayed there, looking. And, after a few minutes, she began to imagine another girl, very like herself, but not exactly the same. The hair a little different, the mouth a little smaller, the lips a little darker. And she could make her look a little older, and a little more. And Siobhán knew. She was able to imagine her mother's face.

She closed her eyes. She could feel her mother's hands holding her up, to grab the conker. She turned and she could see her mother's face. It wasn't clear, it wasn't exact. But it was there, in her head.

'The big one, the big one. Grab it. Yesss!'

And Siobhán felt happy for the first time since her mother had died. But she forgot all about the beautiful woman's message to her father.

Siobhán grew older – fourteen, fifteen. She looked in the mirror every morning and evening. Everybody noticed, and thought that Siobhán was admiring her own beauty. But nobody minded, because Siobhán was beautiful. Eighteen, nineteen, twenty. More years passed, and Siobhán now had a little girl of her own called Ellen, Siobhán's mother's name.

One day, on the morning of her thirtieth birthday, Siobhán put on her mother's mad green shoes because it was a special day. Then she went with Ellen to visit her father in the big house. Her father brought Ellen for a walk in Saint Anne's. While they were away, Siobhán went upstairs to the bathroom. She looked into the mirror and got a shock. She was looking straight at the beautiful woman she'd met all those years ago in the park. The beautiful woman had been her mother and now, on her birthday, Siobhán looked exactly like her.

She cried.

She heard the front door slamming and Little Ellen ran into the bathroom. She was holding a conker. She stopped when she saw Siobhán.

'Why are you crying, Mammy?' she said.

Siobhán picked her up.

'Sometimes people cry when they're happy,' said Siobhán.

'Can I cry as well then?' said Ellen.

'Yes, love,' said Siobhán.

And Siobhán and Ellen cried until they were soaking wet and laughing.

Siobhán's father walked into the bathroom. He had heard them crying and he looked worried. Suddenly, Siobhán remembered her mother's message, the words she had whispered into her ear all those years ago.

'Put a feather in your knickers, Dad,' she said.

Ellen laughed.

Her father's face went very pale.

'Where did you hear that?' he said.

'A beautiful woman told me to tell you,' said Siobhán.

'Your mother,' said her father. 'She said it to me whenever she thought I was being too serious.'

'Put a feather in your knickers, Granda,' said Ellen.

And he laughed. It was the first time Siobhán had heard him laugh. They went downstairs and made coffee and Siobhán's father told them all about her mother, Ellen's grandmother. He told them about how they'd met – at a bus-stop on Abbey Street. He told them about the first film they'd gone to see together, *Revenge of the Killer Snails*. She loved it, he hated it, and she shoved a piece of popcorn up his nose.

He told them about their wedding day – how the cake fell off the table when they were trying to cut it. He told them everything.

It was dark by the time he stopped talking. He was tired and he was happy. Siobhán was also very tired and happy. And little Ellen was asleep.

And that's the end of the story. Siobhán didn't live happily ever after but she lived a long, long life and she was happy a lot of the time. Her father lived long enough to see Ellen grow into a woman. And what about Ellen? She's mad and funny and beautiful and she cycles around Dublin with a big bag of feathers, looking for men who look too serious.

The Midnight Horse

POEM BY MARGRIT CRUICKSHANK

ILLUSTRATED BY BRIGID COLLINS

DO you ever go on the midnight horse
Up in the sky's vast brightness?
His hooves strike sparks among the stars
And his mane floats out like the Milky Way;
While the old man moon, a pale balloon,
Bleaches the world with his whiteness?

The Midnight Horse

A ruby glow in the sky surrounds you,
Beneath you a city of brilliant light.
Neon-lit roads are intersecting,
Black snakes sleep where rivers are flowing,
Floodlit buildings whose grace astounds you
Rear up into the night.

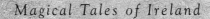

Soon you're off over land where the lights are few –
Small bright sparks in the landscape's darkness,
Windows with warm little lives inside.
But your horse gallops on with no break in its stride!
Cars and trucks move like tiny glowworms
Past fields in the moonlight with hard black edges.

Then out to the sea over waves a-glitter,
The moonlight a path of broad invitation
To follow its silver trail to the end of the world.
Your strong, sleek horse, your horse of darkness
Gallops along, eyes flashing, hooves sparking,
You feel his power, his strength, his magic,
You're part of him, night's mighty stallion,
And the moon seems to wink in the sky.

As you turn for home over seascapes glittering,
Over dark landmass, city lights a-flickering,
Sleep casts its spell and your head is nodding,
Your hands in his mane relax their holding . . .
And he tumbles you off in your very own bed
With a sudden shake of his noble head.

You dream of that ride through the cold night air;
You smell the dust in his wild, brown hair;
And you fall asleep, hoping he'll be there
When you wake up again in the morning.